When Mama Mirabelle Comes Home...

by Douglas Wood
Illustrations by Andy Wagner

NATIONAL GEOGRAPHIC
WASHINGTON, DC

FOR VALERIE AND HUMPHREY, WHO MAKE HOME MY FAVORITE PLACE IN THE WORLD. DW

A National Geographic Kids Entertainment and C Beebies and King Rollo Films Co-production.

Book design by Bea Jackson.

Photo credits
pp 20-21 Lion: Judy Foldetta/iStockphoto; Elephant: Luka Esenko/iStockphoto; Horse: Eileen Hart/iStockphoto
pp 22-23 Geese: WizData, inc./Shutterstock; Sheep: Tommy Martin/iStockphoto; Dolphins: Marco Crisari/iStockphoto
pp 26-27 Bear: Gerry Ellis/Digital Vision

Founded in 1888, the National Geographic Society is one of the largest nonprofit scientific and educational organizations in the world. It reaches more than 285 million people worldwide each month through its official journal, NATIONAL GEOGRAPHIC, and its four other magazines; the National Geographic Channel; television documentaries; radio programs; films; books; videos and DVDs; maps; and interactive media. National Geographic has funded more than 8,000 scientific research projects and supports an education program combating geographic illiteracy.

For more information, please call 1-800-NGS LINE (647-5463) or write to the following address:

NATIONAL GEOGRAPHIC SOCIETY
1145 17th Street N.W., Washington, D.C. 20036-4688 U.S.A.

Visit us online at www.nationalgeographic.com/books

Librarians and Teachers, visit www.ngchildrensbooks.com

For information about special discounts for bulk purchases, please contact National Geographic Books Special Sales: ngspecsales@ngs.org

For rights or permissions inquiries, please contact National Geographic Books Subsidiary Rights: ngbookrights@ngs.org

Library of Congress Cataloging-in-Publication Information is available from the Library of Congress upon request.
Trade ISBN: 978-1-4263-0194-0
Library Binding ISBN: 978-1-4263-0195-7

Printed in Mexico

IT WAS ONE OF THOSE LONG HOT DAYS that seem to go on forever. Even the droopy branches of the acacia tree looked bored.

"What do you want to do?" Karla the zebra asked Max the elephant.

"I don't know. What do you want to do?" Max asked Karla.

“There’s nothing to do on this whole wide savanna,” said Bo the cheetah.

“You can say that again,” said Karla. “Nothing. Absolutely nothing.”

The three friends wandered aimlessly from one patch of shade to another.

"I miss Mama Mirabelle," said Bo.

"Me too," said Karla.

"Me three," said Max.

“When Mama Mirabelle comes home,” said Max, “I’m going to run in the sprinkler!”

“When Mama Mirabelle comes home,” said Karla, “we’re going to play hide-and-seek!”

"When Mama Mirabelle comes home," said Bo, "I'm going to race her to to our favorite tree!"

Kip, Flip, and Chip had their own idea of what they would do with Mama Mirabelle when she came home!

“When Mama comes home, we’ll take a hike to visit the swallows in their nests,” said Karla.

"Hey!" said Karla. "When Mama Mirabelle comes home, maybe she'll take us on one of her whirlwind tours!"

"We could visit our cousins!" said Max.

"And our friends!" added Bo.

“When we come home from our trip,” suggested Max, “maybe all of the animals we visited could come with us to MOVIE TIME!”

"And this time, we'll be the stars," said Karla proudly.

"I can't wait," said Bo wistfully. "Everything's so much more fun when Mama Mirabelle is home."

"Did someone say my name?" came a voice from not so far away. . . .

"Karla! Bo! My little Maxie!" said Mama. "I missed you more than a camel misses his hump! I'm ready to race or ride, party or play. What would you like to do first?"

Karla, Bo, and Max looked at one another for a long moment. "Nothing," they said. "Absolutely nothing."

And that's just what they did.